COUNT DR[illegible] GETS A SHOCK

Count Dracula climbed out of his coffin.
"All the others have gone," he said
to himself.
"Good. A little peace at last."

"I'll have to make my own supper,"
moaned the Count.
"The ghost always made the supper.
This is no fun, this is no fun at all."
The Count opened one door after another.
"I don't know where anything is.
I can't find any blood to drink.
And there is nothing for me to eat, either."

What a disappointment!
RATS BLOOD WINE
BREAD

"Never mind," said Dracula to himself.
"I don't need the others one little bit.
I want to spend the night all on my own in
my scary castle.
Yes, I was very fed up with the ghost and
F.M. and the werewolf, I really was.
Now it is like it used to be.

Just me, waiting for victims to bite. Waiting for victims to come knocking on my door."

Outside, the four watched Dracula through the window.
"How is he getting on?" whispered the werewolf.

"Don't worry, he looks very fed up indeed," said the ghost.
"As if he were having a sulk."
"Do you think it's time for us to knock on the door?" asked the witch.
"Let's see if he will let us back in."

"I shall play on my own until the victims come," moaned the Count.
"The night is young. Tonight I will play on my own and have fun."

"The Count is not happy," said the ghost.
"Shall we go back?"
"No!" said the werewolf. "Not yet.
Let's wait until we are really welcome
in his castle."

"Let's scare him!" said F.M.
"Let's trick him again," agreed the ghost with a smile. "I would like to haunt Castle Dracula very much indeed."

"So would I," replied the werewolf.
"Brilliant, ghost, well done!"
"I can see that in no time at all, we will be back inside the castle," said the witch.
"And we will have a lot of fun at the same time."

They went to the castle and made a lot of noise.
Dracula could not understand what was going on.

He rushed upstairs but could find nothing.
He ran downstairs but could find nothing there either.
He looked under the stairs. He looked out of the window.

"I heard something. It must be the wind," he said to himself.
"The wind does not scare me, but I wish my friends were here. Sometimes the castle is scary!"

"Hello, Count. Please don't be unhappy. We are back!" said F.M.

"Don't worry. You heard right, we are back. Suddenly we felt that you would like us back in the castle with you."

"Brilliant!" shouted the Count. "It is good to see you. I liked being on my own a lot, but suddenly there was noise all over the castle."

"Did the noise scare you, Count?"
asked the others.
"Scare me! A bit of noise! What nonsense
you talk," said Dracula.
No, it did not scare me one bit."

"Before we agree to stay, Count, I need an answer right now, this very minute," said the werewolf.

"Can the witch live here with us too?"

"Yes," shouted Dracula. "She is very welcome indeed to stay in my castle. You are all my good friends and I want you here."